Where Are You, Little Zack?

Judith Ross Enderle and Stephanie Gordon Tessler

Illustrated by Brian Floca

BRICK   BRACK   THACKERY   LITTLE ZACK

Houghton Mifflin Company
Boston 1997

For information about this and other Houghton Mifflin trade and
reference books and multimedia products, visit The Bookstore
at Houghton Mifflin on the World Wide Web at http://www.hmco.com/trade/.

The text of this book is set in 15.5 pt. Times.
The illustrations are ink and watercolor, reproduced in full color.

Library of Congress Cataloging-in-Publication Data
Enderle, Judith R.
Where are you little Zack? / by Judith Enderle
and Stephanie Gordon Tessler; illustrated by Brian Floca.
p. cm.
Summary: Zack Quack and his brothers take the train to New York City
where Zack gets lost, and the three brothers
are joined by increasing numbers of city folks trying to find him.
ISBN 0-395-73092-9
[1. Ducks — Fiction. 2. Lost children — Fiction. 3. New York (N.Y.) — Fiction.
4. City and town life — Fiction. 5. Counting.]
I. Tessler, Stephanie Gordon. II. Floca, Brian, ill. III. Title.
PZ7.E6965Wh 1997
[E] — dc20 96-15381 CIP AC

Manufactured in the United States of America
HOR 10 9 8 7 6 5 4 3 2 1

To our big Zach Quack. Where are you?
We love you and miss you.

— J.R.E / S.G.T.

For the staff and management at
Kearns and Petrillo Budget Lodgings, Manhattan

— B.F.

The duck brothers: Little Zack, Brick and Brack,
and Thackery Quack
took the number 1 train
on track number 2 to the city.
But —

when the train arrived
at Grand Central Station,
Little Zack Quack was missing!
"Where are you, Little Zack?"
called Brick and Brack, and Thackery Quack.

The 3 duck brothers searched
north, south, east, and west
in Grand Central Station.
They found —

4 frantic commuters.
But no sign of Little Zack Quack.
So —

The 3 duck brothers
and the 4 frantic commuters boarded a bus.

They looked uptown.
They looked downtown.
"Where are you, Little Zack?"
cried Brick and Brack, and Thackery Quack.
They found —

5 friendly taxi drivers.
But no sign of Little Zack Quack.
So —

the 3 duck brothers,
4 frantic commuters, and
5 friendly taxi drivers
sailed to the Statue of Liberty.

MISS ELLIS ISLAND
NEW YORK, N.Y.

They looked up.
They looked down.
They looked around the crown.
"Where are you, Little Zack?"
cried Brick and Brack, and Thackery Quack.
They found —

6 smiling tour guides.
But no sign of Little Zack Quack.
So —

the 3 duck brothers,
4 frantic commuters,
5 friendly taxi drivers, and
6 smiling tour guides
paraded up Park Avenue.

They searched the shops.
They gazed in the galleries.
"Where are you, Little Zack?"
cried Brick and Brack, and Thackery Quack.
They found —

7 solemn sales assistants.
But no sign of Little Zack Quack.
So —

the 3 duck brothers,
4 frantic commuters,
5 friendly taxi drivers,
6 smiling tour guides, and
7 solemn sales assistants
took the subway to see
a baseball game in the Bronx.

They hunted at the hot dog stand.
They searched at the souvenir shop.
"Where are you, Little Zack?"
cried Brick and Brack, and Thackery Quack.
They found —

80,000 excited fans.
But no sign of Little Zack Quack.
So —

the 3 duck brothers,
4 frantic commuters,
5 friendly taxi drivers,
6 smiling tour guides,
7 solemn sales assistants, and
80,000 excited fans
caught the number 9 train
on track number 10 to the country.
And they found —

Little Zack Quack!
"Where were you?"
cried the 3 duck brothers,
4 frantic commuters,
5 friendly taxi drivers,
6 smiling tour guides,
7 solemn sales assistants,
and 80,000 excited fans.

"Looking for you!"
said Little Zack Quack.